H is for Haunted House

A Halloween Alphabet Book

For my Jake, who still wishes every day was Halloween!—T.L.S.

To my two sons, Max and Titus—S.B.

PRICE STERN SLOAN
Published by the Penguin Group
Penguin Group (USA) Inc., 375 Hudson Street, New York, New York 10014, USA
Penguin Group (Canada), 90 Eglinton Avenue East, Suite 700,
Toronto, Ontario M4P 2Y3, Canada
(a division of Pearson Penguin Canada Inc.)
Penguin Books Ltd., 80 Strand, London WC2R 0RL, England
Penguin Group Ireland, 25 St. Stephen's Green, Dublin 2, Ireland
(a division of Penguin Books Ltd.)
Penguin Group (Australia), 250 Camberwell Road, Camberwell, Victoria 3124, Australia
(a division of Pearson Australia Group Pty. Ltd.)
Penguin Books India Pvt. Ltd., 11 Community Centre,
Panchsheel Park, New Delhi—110 017, India
Penguin Group (NZ), 67 Apollo Drive, Rosedale, North Shore 0632, New Zealand
(a division of Pearson New Zealand Ltd.)
Penguin Books (South Africa) (Pty.) Ltd., 24 Sturdee Avenue,
Rosebank, Johannesburg 2196, South Africa

Penguin Books Ltd., Registered Offices:
80 Strand, London WC2R 0RL, England

The scanning, uploading, and distribution of this book via the Internet or via any other means without the permission of the publisher is illegal and punishable by law. Please purchase only authorized electronic editions and do not participate in or encourage electronic piracy of copyrighted materials. Your support of the author's rights is appreciated.

Text copyright © 2010 by Tanya Lee Stone. Illustrations copyright © 2010 by Scott Burroughs. All rights reserved. Published by Price Stern Sloan, a division of Penguin Young Readers Group, 345 Hudson Street, New York, New York 10014. *PSS!* is a registered trademark of Penguin Group (USA) Inc. Manufactured in China.

Library of Congress Control Number: 2009035332

ISBN 978-0-8431-3716-3   10 9 8 7 6 5 4 3 2 1

H is for Haunted House

A Halloween Alphabet Book

by Tanya Lee Stone
illustrated by Scott Burroughs

PSS!
PRICE STERN SLOAN
An Imprint of Penguin Group (USA) Inc.

A is for autumn,
The best time of year.
We have a big party
'Cause Halloween's here!

B is for bats,
'Round and 'round us they fly.
Their black wings flip-flap
As they swoop through the sky.

C is for **costumes,**
And contests with prizes,
For heroes and creatures
In all shapes and sizes.

D is for **dangerous**—
A ghoul grabs my knee.
It's just my big brother,
He'll NEVER scare me!

E is for eyeballs
(They're grapes that we peel).
They slip through our fingers,
We scream and we squeal!

F is for Frankenstein,
Green skin and bolts.
But under that mask
I see Principal Holtz!

G is for ghost.
I don't see them—do you?
Then out from the shadows
They leap and shout . . . BOO!

I is for icky,
Huge spiders that crawl.
Their furry legs scurry
All over that wall!

H is for haunted house,
Cobwebs and creaks,
Old broken windows,
And hair-raising shrieks!

J is for **jack-o-lanterns**
Glowing so bright,
With all kinds of faces
To light up the night.

K is for **knocking**,
Rap-tap on the door.
We're pirates and fairies,
Cats, werewolves, and more.

L is for leaves

Blowing every which way.
They swirl 'round our feet,
Then fly up and away!

CITY PARK

N is for nighttime,
A blanket of dark.
We shine our bright flashlights
To race past the park!

M is for mummy
Wound up in white tape.
It chases behind me,
Until I escape!

O is for owl
Who searches the skies.
He peers from the treetops
With huge, yellow eyes.

P is for potion

That's served with great flair.
Poured out of a pumpkin,
Drink up if you dare!

Q is for **quaking**
Right down to our toes.
But that's just our neighbor
Beneath scary clothes.

R is for R.I.P.,
Marked on a grave.
A chocolate cake tombstone,
Dig in—and be brave!

S is for skeleton
With rattling bones,
Chattering teeth, and
Spine-tingling moans!

T is for "Trick or Treat,"
We yell as we knock.
We go house to house
For block after block.

U is for ugly—
A creepy, green troll.
And right on her nose
Is a big, hairy mole.

V is for vampire,
Dressed all in black.
He bares his sharp fangs
As he flings his cape back!

W is for witches

**Who cast spells and fly
Right by on their broomsticks
And up to the sky.**

X is in eXtra-large
Bag full of loot.
Tonight lots of candy,
Tomorrow—just fruit.

Y is for yikes!
I see golden eyes glow.
What's that by the door?
Just a kitty I know.

Z is for zombie,
Stomp-clomp through the night.
Oh, look! It's just Daddy,
To tuck me in tight.